# TEEN TITANS

# Blinde[d] the Light

By J. Torres

Illustrated by
Kevin MacKenzie

Scholastic Inc.

New York    Toronto    London    Auckland    Sydney
Mexico City    New Delhi    Hong Kong    Buenos Aires

ISBN: 0-439-69635-6

Published by Scholastic Inc.
SCHOLASTIC and associated logos are trademarks and/or registered trademarks of Scholastic Inc.

12 11 10 9 8 7 6 5 4 3 2    5 6 7 8 9/0

Designed by Carisa Swenson
Printed in the U.S.A.
First printing, March 2005

# Chapter One

## Here Comes Trouble

They call me Beast Boy. Okay, I call myself that, too. That's because I can transform into any creature in the animal kingdom, including some that are extinct.

The only thing is, I'm green. Like, all over. Meaning when I use my superpowers to change into a black panther . . . the jungle cat I turn into is green. A green panther.

When I want to transform into a pink flamingo . . . I become a green flamingo. Blue whale . . . green whale. Gray owl . . . green owl. White-tailed deer . . . green deer, tail and all. Red Spitting Cobra . . . green. Greenback turtle . . . uh, green. Goldfish . . . green. Zebra . . . two-tone green stripes.

Spider, sheep, shark, stegosaurus . . . green, green, green, green. You get the picture!

Speaking of pictures, this is the story of what happened when my teammates and I went to see *Super Ninja Fury: The Movie.*

By *teammates* I mean the Teen Titans:

Cyborg, my half-human, half-robot, and all-cool buddy with the sonic cannon.

Starfire, a superpowered alien girl who flies and

fires energy bolts from her hands.

Raven, whose dark personality matches the black energy she uses to do all sorts of mysterious tricks.

Robin, our own little super ninja with all sorts of cool martial arts moves and weapons.

So there we were, the first people in line to see the first ever screening of *Super Ninja Fury: The Movie.* You know *Super Ninja Fury* for the Game

Station, right? You've played the game, now see the movie!

Anyway, we got to the theater super early and had been waiting hours. The sun was still up when we got in line, but now it was dark out and the streetlights were on. But it was worth it because we were the first five in a line of hundreds of people that snaked down the street and around the corner.

Note that I say "were." As in past tense. Because as we stood there waiting to be ushered into the movie theater, Cyborg noticed something weird.

"Yo!" Cy yelled. "Check out the lights on the marquee."

"What is the meaning of this on-and-off thing that they are doing?" asked Starfire.

In fact, all the lights up and down the whole street were doing the on-and-off thing.

"Something tells me these flickering lights mean trouble," said Robin.

Just then, the emergency alarm on his

T-Communicator went off with a *BEEP BEEP BEEP!*

We all gathered around Robin as he pushed a button and looked into his communicator.

Robin was right — the flickering lights meant trouble. The green hair on the back of my green neck stood up at what he said next . . .

"Dr. Light is back."

# Chapter Two

## Dr. Who?

**W**ho is Dr. Light, you ask? He's a man who has a special high-tech suit that can generate intense light and shoot laser beams. He's a man who uses these superpowers to destroy things. He also likes to steal stuff that's so not his. The Teen Titans have dealt with him once or twice in the past.

In short, Dr. Light is one of the bad guys.

"He's back, Titans," grunted Robin. "And of course he's up to no good!"

"So, exactly what is he up to?" asked Cyborg.

"Is he making the lights do the on–and–off thing?" asked Starfire.

Robin spoke as he attached his communicator

to his Utility Belt: "Dr. Light is trashing the hydro-electric generator. We should stop him before he causes a citywide blackout." Robin sounded a bit reluctant.

Now, I know what you're thinking. Robin was thinking it, too. Here we are, the first in line to see *Super Ninja Fury: The Movie*. Some stupid villain starts making trouble. It's our job to stop super-villains from making trouble. So we have to lose our primo place in line to see *Super Ninja Fury: The Movie*. Yeah. Being a teenage crime fighter sometimes has its downside.

"Aw, man! What about the movie?" I asked.

It was at that point that Raven gave me the look. What look? The look. You know the look your mother gives you when you say something that you shouldn't have? That look.

Just when I was sure Cyborg was going to give me the father version of the look, he said, "You're right! We've been waiting for hours! We can't give up our place in line."

"No worries," Robin said. "Starfire and I can easily take care of Dr. Lightweight!"

"I'm sure you two are more than capable, but can I still go with you?" Raven requested. "I'd rather deal with Light than this lineup."

"No, you guys wait here," replied Robin. "If we're not back before they let the line in, save us some seats. No super-villain's going to keep me from

seeing *Super Ninja Fury: The Movie.*"

"Please do not forget to purchase me some popped corn! But no buttery-flavored liquid topping — I prefer ketchup!" Starfire told Raven.

"Have it your way," Raven said with a sigh.

Starfire and Robin joined hands. Then Starfire took off into the air, carrying Robin. Yes, she's a girl but she's that strong. Alien girls from her planet are way stronger than most boys I know on this world. So, if you're an Earth boy, you might want to think twice before challenging Star to a game of dodgeball or an arm wrestle.

Everyone in line cheered as they watched Robin and Starfire fly into the sky. The movie hadn't started yet, but they were already getting quite a show!

I was glad Robin suggested the rest of us stay in line. I figured he and Starfire should be able to handle Dr. Light — no problem. Little did I know what the evil dude had in store for them. . . .

# Chapter Three

## Come Fly With Me

Okay, his name is Robin. The robin is a type of bird. Trust me, I know my birds. Despite his name, Robin can't fly. Oh, he can jump, flip, and tumble with some serious hang time in between — but he can't fly.

Cyborg can't fly, either, but he can get some big air when he does a running leap. Those robotic legs of his are way powerful. He can even leap tall buildings in a single bound.

Then there's Raven. Another one with a bird name. She can sort of fly, but not really. What she does is called *levitation*. She kind of . . . floats and glides. Raven's good at it and is able to get up fairly high and move quite quickly when she levitates. It looks like flying, so same dif, actually.

Now, I can definitely fly. But to do so I have to take the form of something with wings. Well, except penguins. Or ostriches. Or the extinct dodo. Not all birds can fly, even though they have wings. (See? I told you I knew my birds!)

But the expert flyer of the Teen Titans is Starfire. Everyone from her planet can fly. She's from a planet called Tamaran, by the way. I know my birds, but planets not so much, so let's just say Tamaran is far, far away.

So Robin can't fly. But he often gets an airlift from Starfire. They have this move where they join hands like trapeze artists. He says they "lock" hands for this move. She says they're "holding" hands. Tee-hee.

In any case, she carries him hanging beneath her as she flies. This makes Robin look like an acrobat swinging through the air. Or like a kid dangling from monkey bars. You get the picture.

High in the sky, Star and Robbie were able to see

that the lights were out in a section of the city.

"See that dark area over there?" Robin asked. "That's where the hydroelectric generator is located."

Robin's geography is solid. He knows where and what everything is on the map. "And since that's where the hydroelectric generator is, that's where we'll find Dr. Light," he continued.

Starfire flew them as quickly as she could in that very direction.

# Chapter Four

## Now You See Him . . .

At the hydroelectric generator, Dr. Light gleefully fired lasers from his fingertips at some machinery. These machines were used to create electricity with waterpower.

The super-villain was about to destroy the generator and cause power failures all across the city. It was already dark in the area. Star and Robbie knew they should proceed with caution. Who knew what danger awaited them in the darkness?

"This is where I get off," said Robin. That was Starfire's cue to drop him.

"Woo-hoo!" Robin cried as he fell. He went free-falling like a skydiver, then did a midair tuck and roll. Finally, he grabbed a corner of his cape in

each hand and used it as a parachute.

On his way down, Robin expertly steered toward the hydroelectric generator. He made sure to land inside the restricted zone's fence. His feet hit the ground with a *SPLASH!*

"Splash?" he said curiously. Looking down, he noticed that the pavement was wet — although it had been sunny all week.

"Robin! Over here!" cried Starfire. She had landed a few yards away and found something odd: a stream of water flowing from the main building.

"This is a leak?" wondered Starfire.

"This is a *lead*," replied Robin.

He ran toward the main building. He knew that if they followed the water, they'd find the villain.

Inside, Dr. Light was snickering at the damage he had just done. Water was gushing from one of the turbines he'd blasted. The turbine needed water to generate electricity.

"Mwa-ha-ha-ha! Soon they'll all be at my mercy," cackled Dr. Light.

He was so busy laughing and admiring his nasty work that he didn't notice Robin and Starfire sneaking up behind him.

"You're not very bright, are you?" Robin asked.

"The Teen Titans!" sneered Dr. Light. "But . . . there are only two of you? Where are the rest?"

"They're busy!" replied Robin. "But they asked me to give you this!"

With that, Robin kicked water in Dr. Light's face. This was his trick to distract the villain while he made his move. As Light angrily wiped the water from his eyes, Robin threw a metal ball his way.

This silver ball is about the size of a jawbreaker. It's a small package with a big surprise. As the ball

flew through the air, it split in half and released an expanding net!

The net covered Dr. Light, trapping him.

"What's this?" the captured criminal cried.

As he struggled, Robin and Starfire carefully approached.

"It would be wise for you to surrender now, Doctor," Starfire suggested politely.

"Yeah, make this easier on yourself. Put your hands in the air," added Robin.

Dr. Light did begin to raise his hands. But, of course, he wasn't going to surrender that easily. A sneaky smile spread across his face. The palms of his raised hands began to glow.

Before Robin and Starfire knew it, the scheming super-villain sent two deadly rays of light in their direction: *ZAP! ZAP!*

# Chapter Five

## . . . Now You Don't!

Luckily, Dr. Light wasn't only a bad man, he was also a bad shot. He missed both his targets. But the rays of light he fired were like powerful lasers. They hit the wall with a *BOOM! BOOM!* The wall crumbled like a cracker!

Starfire cartwheeled one way to avoid the chunks of falling concrete. Robin somersaulted the other way to keep from being crushed. As both heroes landed on their feet, the room suddenly went dark.

Dr. Light had knocked out the lights by blasting a control panel on another wall with more laser fire. It was bad enough with the choking dust clouds in the air and dangerous rubble everywhere. Now Robin and Starfire were lost in a pitch-black void.

"Starfire! Are you all right?" called out Robin, coughing on the dust.

"I am just fine, thank you," replied Starfire from somewhere in the shadows. "How are you?"

"Feeling stupid," answered Robin. "I should have known Light wouldn't give up just like that!"

Robin took a penlight out of his Utility Belt. He used it to scan the inky darkness for Starfire. In one corner of the room, he spotted what looked like two large fireflies. They were Starfire's eyes!

Then Robin thought he saw something move

quickly across the dark room. "There! I think Light ran through that door!"

The two Titans dashed toward the door. There was more blackness in the next room, so they stopped at the entrance.

"Get ready, Starfire," commanded Robin.

He took a small metal rod from his Utility Belt and pulled at both ends of it, revealing his weapon of choice: the bo staff. Within seconds, the five-inch metal rod became a pole five feet long!

Starfire made a fist and it began to glow green like her firefly eyes. "I am ready," she said.

Robin stood on the right-hand side of the door-way. Starfire was on the opposite side. They exchanged silent looks, confirming their next moves. He was going to go in first. She was going to watch his back.

Robin peered into the darkness. The green glow from Starfire's fist allowed him to see where Dr. Light was waiting for them inside the next room. Unfortunately, Dr. Light could also see Robin.

"Look into the light," the villain said, before he struck with a *FLASH!*

"Argh!" Robin cried out in pain.

"Aieee!" screamed Starfire.

Dr. Light had hit them with a burst of light so bright that it stung their eyes. It also blinded them long enough for him to escape. They couldn't see where he went. They couldn't see anything. But they could hear him cackling as he left them in the dark.

# Chapter Six

## Someone's Going to Pay

**W**hile Robin and Starfire were waiting to regain their sight, we were still waiting in line to see *Super Ninja Fury: The Movie*. We'd been in line half the day. Now it was nightfall and almost time for the movie to start!

You could sense the excitement in the air. Everyone in line was dying to see *Super Ninja Fury: The Movie*. Well, everyone except Raven.

"Maybe it wasn't such a good idea to let those guys go after Dr. Light without us," she finally said after standing in silence the whole time since Robin and Starfire had left.

Raven likes to meditate. Sometimes she says her mantra (or chant), "*Azarath, Metrion, Zinthos,*" over and over again. I thought she was meditating. Really, she was just being quiet. She gets that way sometimes. I don't know how she does it. Stay quiet for so long, I mean.

"I bet they're kicking Dr. Light's butt as we speak!" I said excitedly. "Maybe even kicking butt like super ninjas full of fury!"

"Could be . . . but yelling it in my ear won't make it true," replied Raven with a frown.

Okay, maybe I said it kind of loudly.

The lights up and down the street started to do the on-and-off thing again.

"Maybe Raven's right," said Cyborg, looking up at the flickering marquee lights.

Then his left eye started to do the on-and-off thing!

When Cy's red eye flashes, it usually means there's an emergency. And usually, it's Robin calling in the red alert. So, Robbie was using Cyborg's eye while his were still seeing spots.

"Dude! Light got us good," said Robin over his communicator. He sounded angry.

"What happened? Are you all right?" asked Cyborg. He sounded concerned.

"Well, you can say that we were blinded by the light," said Starfire. She sounded . . . cute.

They quickly told us what had happened, and explained that they couldn't see properly. In their present condition, it was too dangerous to walk — never mind fly anywhere! So we had to go after Dr. Light now.

"I'm already tracking him," said Cyborg as he punched some keys on the computer in his fore-arm. A mini-satellite dish popped out, pointed upward, spun around, and scanned the skies. Cy hit a couple more keys.

"Got him!" he yelled. "He's in City Section 12!"

"Section 12," repeated Raven. "That's where the power plant is."

Cyborg wagged a metal finger at me. "You stay put!" he said. "Raven and I will take care of getting some payback for Star and Robbie."

"No arguments from me!" I said. "You want butter on your popcorn, too?"

"No popcorn," he replied. "But some Choco Nutz or Smelly Jellies would be nice!"

"What about you, Rave?" I asked.

"Um . . . some black licorice," Raven replied. "Please."

"Okay, I'll get the goodies while you guys get the baddie!"

I was surprised that Raven agreed to let me stay in line. I was happy to keep our places, of course. I just thought she'd be all "this is pointless" and "how useless" about it.

I guess she secretly wanted to see *Super Ninja Fury: The Movie* as much as the rest of us. As much as everyone in line who were now cheering as they watched Cyborg bound off and Raven levitate away.

As I watched them zoom off to the power plant to get Dr. Light back for what he did to Robin and Starfire, it suddenly hit me. . . .

"I DON'T HAVE ENOUGH MONEY TO PAY FOR ALL THAT CANDY!"

# Chapter Seven

## The Speed of Light

At Jump City's main power station, Dr. Light was having fun severing cables and destroying electrical equipment, knowing that all across the city people were being plunged into darkness. Soon, all of them would have no choice but to look to the light — Dr. Light.

As the bad guy made a mess of the power station, the good guys made their way toward the scene of the crime.

There, a frantic security guard stood at the edge of the driveway. "Help! Please!" he yelled. "He's destroying the place!"

"Don't worry, sir," replied Cyborg. "We're on it!"

The driveway leading from the street up to the

power plant facility is about 150 to 200 yards long. That's three or four Olympic-size-pool lengths. It took Cyborg about three crashing jumps to get from one end of the driveway to the other.

Meanwhile, Raven preferred a quieter approach: "*Azarath, Metrion, Zinthos,*" she chanted as she stood standing behind the guardhouse.

Her words conjured up a mysterious void beneath her feet. It started as a tiny dark dot under her left heel and expanded until it was about as big as a hula hoop. She sank into this black hole and disappeared. She was using her dark powers to teleport herself to where Light was.

Inside the vast power station, Dr. Light continued his destruction of public property. Sparks flew everywhere. Clouds of smoke polluted the air. And where there was smoke, there were generators on fire!

"Ha-ha-ha! It's getting hot in here!" shouted Dr. Light.

On the other side of a steel door, Cyborg could hear everything Light was saying.

*BAM!*

He kicked the door open and confronted the snickering super-villain.

"It's time to cool off!" Cyborg barked.

"Another Teen Titan!" sneered Dr. Light.

At the same time, a shadowy spot formed on the floor behind Light. It quickly expanded from the size of a dime to the size of tractor tire. Raven rose from its darkness.

"Make that two Titans!" Raven said, startling Dr. Light.

Her stealthy entrance distracted the villain, giving Cyborg enough time to break out his sonic cannon with a *CH-CHIK CH-CHIK*. He was all attitude as he pointed it at Dr. Light.

"Come quietly or I get loud," Cyborg said.

By *loud* Cyborg meant the big *BOOM* of his sonic cannon. When he fires that thing, it sounds like thunder inside your head. That's loud!

But the threat of punishment to his eardrums didn't seem to faze Dr. Light. "Don't you know?" he asked. "Light travels faster than sound!"

Dr. Light's suit quickly began to glow white-hot. Cyborg and Raven remembered what had happened to Robin and Starfire. When Light's suit began to go superbright, Cyborg and Raven covered their eyes.

*FLASH!*

When the light faded, Cyborg and Raven looked up. But now the villain was nowhere to be seen. . . .

# Chapter Eight

## Fully Charged

"Nice try, Dr. Light!" yelled Cyborg as he kept his head down. "Did you really think you'd get away with that trick twice?"

"Uh, Cyborg . . ." said Raven. "He's gone."

Cyborg slowly raised his head. "Hey! Where'd he go?" he asked.

"I didn't see, either," replied Raven. "I had my hood pulled down."

Suddenly, the two Titans heard an explosion. *BOOM!* They both turned in the direction of the noise. "There he goes!" they said.

Cyborg and Raven continued deeper into the power station. Cyborg took the lead. Without thinking, he zipped past equipment Dr. Light had laser-blasted. He darted in and out of clouds of smoke, making it hard for Raven to keep up. He was going so fast that he hardly noticed all the sparks flying in the air.

"Watch where you're going!" Raven shouted.

She couldn't keep up with his powerful robotic legs. And she couldn't see up ahead because of all the smoke. She needed a better vantage point.

"*Azarath, Metrion, Zinthos!*" Raven chanted.

She levitated upward. She had hoped to spot Dr. Light, but instead she saw something that made her heart sink even as she floated higher.

Cyborg was headed for a severed electrical cable that was violently thrashing about like an angry snake!

"Cyborg! Stop!" she yelled.

He couldn't hear her. He couldn't see the dangerous live wire, either. He was running blindly toward it through clouds of smoke!

"*Azarath, Metrion, Zinthos!*" Raven chanted once again.

Black blobs of energy flew out of each of her outstretched hands. As they shot through the air toward Cyborg and the deadly cable, they began to change shape, turning into a pair of giant black hands!

The left hand swooped down and grabbed Cyborg by the ankle. *CRASH!* Down went Cyborg.

The right hand grabbed the hissing cable like a bird snatching a worm in its beak.

"Ow!" Cyborg cried, lying facedown on the ground. "Who the . . . ?"

"Sorry, that was me," confessed Raven.

He was about to get mad at her. Then he heard the *BZZT BZZT* sound of the live wire up ahead. The smoke cleared as Raven landed beside him.

"Oh . . ." said Cyborg. "I guess I owe you one."

"Look before you leap from now on and we're even," replied Raven. "Now, where's Dr. Light?"

The two of them felt a gust of wind. They turned toward the cool draft and saw a gaping hole in the wall. Through the blasted section, they could see Dr. Light outside, standing between two electrical towers with a crackling downed power line in each hand.

"What does he think he's doing?" asked Raven.

"Whatever he's up to . . . don't try that at home, kids!" replied Cyborg.

Raven had just saved Cyborg from being fried by a single live wire. But Dr. Light held two of the dangerous things in his hands!

"Yes! Yes! YES!" cried Dr. Light maniacally.

His power suit began to glow white-hot again. It was absorbing deadly energy!

"No way! He's . . . he's charging up his suit!" exclaimed Cyborg.

"But isn't that too much power?" asked Raven.

Dr. Light dropped the cables. He stared at the smoke rising from his hands and his suit and his entire body. He shimmered with power.

A sinister smile came across his face as he looked up at the Titans.

"I feel positively charged up!" he shouted.

His clenched fists crackled with energy. He pointed them at Cyborg and Raven. He cackled, and . . . *FWOOM! FWOOM!*

Dr. Light fired two massive beams of light at the two Titans. *BOOM! BOOM!* They both hit the ground. The entire building trembled as if an earthquake hit it.

Cyborg yelled out, "Incoming!"

Raven tried to get the words out: "*Azarath, Me-trion, Zin —*"

But they disappeared under a mountain of bricks.

Dr. Light then disappeared into the night. . . .

# Chapter Nine

## Meanwhile . . .

The theater was late letting us in to see *Super Ninja Fury: The Movie*. They said something about "technical difficulties." I didn't mind waiting longer because Robin, Starfire, Cyborg, and Raven hadn't gotten back yet. It was a different story for the other people in line.

"S-N-F! S-N-F! S-N-F!" they all chanted.

This made the people working at the movie theater nervous. The lady in the box office even closed the window. One of the ushers asked me to "do something." He was worried the crowd would storm the theater.

So, I did that only thing I could think of . . . I turned into a tyrannosaurus rex!

That freaked them out. The people went from chanting to screaming their heads off.

So I went for cute and transformed into a puppy.

"Aww, isn't it cute?" a young girl said. I ran up and down the line barking playfully and happily wagging my tail. Cute worked for this crowd. They forgot about the extra waiting time.

And I forgot about my friends.

I didn't realize that at the same time, Dr. Light was shocking Cyborg and Raven with his powered-up suit.

Meanwhile, Robin and Starfire had regained their sight but were busy preventing a flood at the hydroelectric generator.

There was no sign of any of them by the time the line began to move. I figured no news was good news. So I stuck with our original plan of saving everyone a seat.

*Hoo-boy!* I thought. *I'm about to see* Super Ninja Fury: The Movie!

I made a beeline for the best seats in the house. Some people were upset that I was hogging so many seats. Others were scared of me. How would you react if you saw a large green octopus saving four seats in a movie theater?

Not long after I sat down, the lights went out. I wondered why they turned them off so soon. Most people were still being let into the theater. A lot of people were tripping in the dark.

"Ouch! My foot!"

"Get off me, you clumsy jerk!"

"Watch where you're falling!"

"I can't see a thing!"

Some dude tripped over his girlfriend and spilled his drink all over me. As I tried to dry off, I realized that the movie hadn't started. There weren't even previews or commercials playing.

Maybe they *hadn't* turned off the lights. Maybe this was another "technical difficulty." Maybe this was like the on-and-off thing all over again!

I immediately turned into a bat so I could use sonar to find my way in the dark and fly over everybody.

I quickly reached the lobby, but there were no lights on there, either. The popcorn machine wasn't working. Looking out the window, I noticed the entire street was without power!

The other Titans had obviously failed to stop Dr. Light.

# Chapter Ten

## Titans Together

It was almost as dark outside as it was inside. The marquee wasn't doing the on-and-off thing anymore. Neither were the streetlights. Everything was just off.

The only lights around were from the cars honking their horns. With the traffic lights out, it was chaotic for the drivers. I'm sure there was all kinds of chaos all over the city.

*That's what Dr. Light wanted all along!* I thought.

But I did't know why he wanted the city in such a mess. As I said before, Dr. Light enjoys using his superpowers to destroy things and steal stuff. Maybe the blackout was about turning off alarm systems so he could rob banks and jewelry stores!

I didn't have time to figure out his motive. I had to stop him. Or go looking for the other Titans.

I was so confused! I didn't know what I should do first! Save my teammates or stop the villain?

The answer came when I saw an eerie glow down the street.

It was Dr. Light marching up the street as if he owned it. His suit was shimmering in a strange way. He almost looked like a ghost.

"Citizens of Jump City! Look to the light!" he said in a creepy voice. "Bring me all your riches and make me your supreme ruler, and I will bring you out of this darkness!"

He then shot off laser fire, shattering store windows. *CRASH! CRASH!*

"If not, it's lights out for you — permanently!" he threatened onlookers.

"So that's what his game is," I said before turning into a rhinoceros.

I charged toward him as fast as I could.

With a wave of his hand, Dr. Light surrounded himself in a yellow force field.

I hit the sunlike bubble with a *WHAM!* It felt like I ran into a brick wall.

Light dropped his protective shield. He then clenched his fist and aimed at me.

*ZAP!* He fired at me, but I turned into a frog and leaped left.

*ZAP!* I turned into a rabbit and hopped right.

*ZAP!* I turned into a kangaroo and jumped straight up.

I was fast . . . but Light was faster. He got me on the way down. *ZAP!* A laser blast to the pouch sent me flying into a bus shelter with a *SMASH!*

"Oww . . . that really hurt," I moaned. "How am I supposed to stop this guy on my own?"

A shadow fell on me. I thought it was Dr. Light there to finish me off.

"You're not going to stop him on your own," a familiar voice said. "We are here to help!"

"Robin!" I shouted in delight. "And Starfire!"

"We apologize for our late arrival," said Starfire. She extended her hand to help me up.

"And I'm sorry I didn't think this through," added Robin. "We should've gone after Dr. Light as a team from the beginning!"

"Yeah . . . besides, with the power out like this," said another familiar voice from behind us, "no one's seeing *Super Ninja Fury: The Movie*, anyway."

It was Cyborg! And Raven!

Right behind them, however, was Dr. Light. He held out both hands and they began to glow super bright. I knew what was coming next.

"Look out! He's right behind you!" I screamed.

I covered my head with my arms and closed my eyes. I thought I was toast. We were toast. But I heard the blast . . . and didn't feel a thing.

When I opened my eyes, I saw we were inside a force field of our own — a black bubble Raven used to protect us. Dr. Light stood outside our shadowy shield shaking an angry fist.

"Neat trick, huh?" asked Cyborg. "She also used it to save us at the power plant when Light brought the building down on us."

"Now, for our next trick," said Raven. "Let's go get Dr. Light."

"Yes!" said Robin. "Together as a team!"

We huddled in a circle and listened to Raven's plan of attack.

"What's the matter, children? Afraid of the light?" taunted the super-villain.

Raven dropped the shield.

Robin yelled, "TITANS . . . GO!"

We scattered in different directions.

Robin threw his birdarang at Dr. Light. The villain dodged it easily enough. He laughed, thinking Robin had missed.

I turned into a porcupine and shot my quills at him. He threw up his force field once again to protect himself. Inside the yellow bubble, he continued to laugh at us.

But that was exactly where we wanted him!

Cyborg broke out his sonic cannon. Starfire charged up her hands. They both took aim at Dr. Light behind his shield.

*SHOOM!* went Starfire's starbolts.

*BOOM!* went Cyborg's sonic cannon.

*SHOOM!*

*BOOM!*

Dr. Light stood confidently within his force field. He continued to laugh like a madman. But Cyborg and Starfire didn't stop firing.

*SHOOM!*

*BOOM!*

The force field flickered — yes, it did the on-and-off thing. Dr. Light looked worried. He patted his power suit all over, looking for the problem. The problem wasn't the suit — it was the power. He was running out of it!

Cyborg and Starfire stopped shooting.

"Give up yet?" asked Cyborg.

"Yes, it would be in your best interest to surrender now," suggested Starfire.

But Dr. Light was stubborn — most super-villains are. He dropped his force field and started firing lasers at all of us.

He aimed for Starfire but she just flew out of its way. His blast hit a fire hydrant and sent water gushing out onto the street.

His second shot was meant for Cyborg. It wasn't as strong as his last blast, so Cyborg just stood there with his hands on his hips. He puffed out his chest and took the hit without flinching.

"Boo-ya!" Cy yelled. "That didn't hurt a bit."

Strike three came at me. It was even weaker

because Dr. Light was running out of juice. I went armadillo on him so when it hit, it only felt like someone poking my hard leathery hide.

"This light's starting to dim, Titans," said Robin. "It's time to put it out!"

Dr. Light's suit began to lose its glow. Smoke rose from his fingertips.

"*Azarath, Metrion, Zinthos!*" chanted Raven.

Dr. Light's shadow began to quiver oddly. The villain looked down at it and began to panic. His whole body trembled as a familiar-looking black hole opened at his feet. Slowly but surely, Dr. Light was swallowed up by the shadow.

"No!" he cried. "Please! I'm afraid of the dark! NOOOOO!"

We gathered around the dark portal.

"Don't worry, your jail cell will have sufficient lighting," said Raven.

She teleported Dr. Light to the Jump City Penitentiary.

"That should teach him," said Cyborg.

"That should teach us," replied Robin. "We do everything as a team from now on!"

"Hooray! We shall do everything as a team forevermore!" cheered Starfire.

"If we hurry up," I added, "we can even catch a late screening of *Super Ninja Fury: The Movie* as a team!"

Raven gave me the look again. Yeah, that look.

"First," she asked, "don't we need to help restore power before anyone can watch any movies?"

"You're right," I said. "No electricity, no *Super Ninja Fury!* Good call!"

"And then," Raven continued, "shouldn't we fix the other damage Dr. Light did?"

I looked around and saw the busted store

windows, the damaged bus shelter, the street flooded by the broken fire hydrant. . . .

"But that could take us all night!" I whined.

"If it does, it does," Raven replied. "Crying about it won't get it done faster. Let's get started."

"Fine," I said. "I just hope you don't come up with any other bright ideas."

# TITANS EAST ACTION FIGURES.
# KICKING EVIL WHERE IT COUNTS.